D0490847

This book belongs to

....

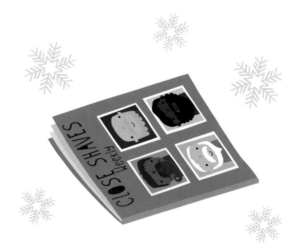

Copyright © 2019

make believe ideas ltd

The Wilderness, Berkhamsted, Hertfordshire, HP4 2AZ, UK.

All rights reserved. No part of this publication may be reproduced,
stored in a retrieval system, or transmitted in any form or by any means,
electronic, mechanical, photocopying, recording, or otherwise, without
the prior written permission of the copyright owner.

www.makebelieveideas.com

Written by Rosie Greening.
Illustrated by Dawn Machell.

Have Yourself a Hairy Little Christmas

Written by **Rosie Greening** · Illustrated by **Dawn Machell**

make
believe
ideas

One morning at **Elf's barber shop**,
Santa's ready for the **chop**.

He says,

"I'd like a brand-new style!"

"Of course," the elf says with a smile.

CLOSE SHAVES Weekly

First, Elf makes a *beard* that's **green**,

and **grows** some carrots, peas and *beans*.

Phew!

Then, Elf **knits** right on the spot,
but Santa moans, **"This beard's too hot!"**

Next, Elf finds some **twinkly lights** and makes a *beard* that's **big** and **bright**.

Santa says, **"It's nice to see, but lights look better on a tree!"**

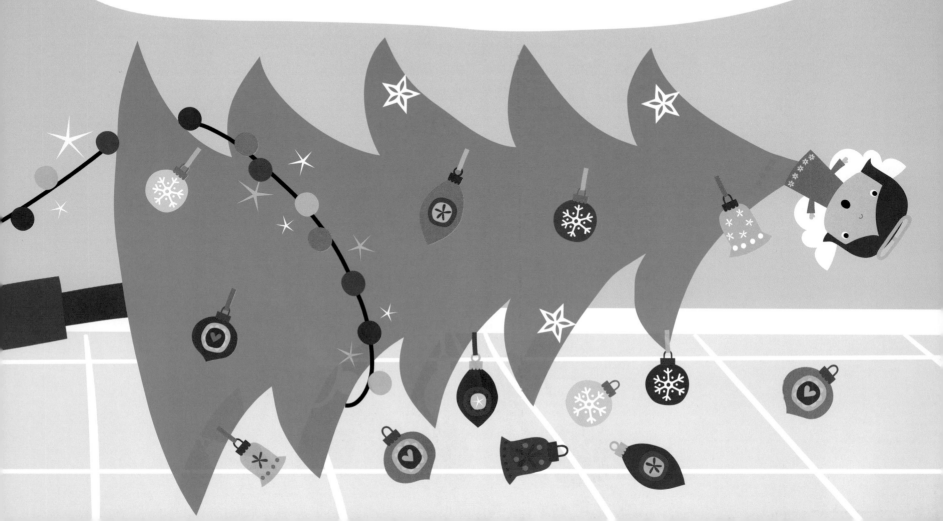

They **sculpt** a **reindeer** out of hair,
but that *beard* just makes people stare.

Elf brings out some coloured **dye** and gives some **rainbow** *beards* a try.

Santa says,
"They're not quite right.

L t's try **b** **r** **th t's NOT so bright!"**

The next **beard** is the **perfect** size,
but then a **MOUSE** jumps out . . .

"Surprise!"

So Elf glues on some
yummy treats
(which hungry Santa quickly eats).

Elf says, "**Frozen beards are nice!**" and makes a **crunchy** *beard* of **ice**.

"Brrrrr!"

"**Much too chilly!**" Santa thinks, and warms up with a nice, **hot drink.**

Santa likes the **plaits** a lot . . .
until he gets into a **knot**.

Elf makes a **flower** *beard* with ease,
but *roses* just make Santa **sneeze!**

"Atchoo!"

Now Elf's ideas are running low,
he **sprays** the *beard* with
Grow 'n' Flow.

The hair soon **fills** the barber shop,

and Santa has to cry out . . .

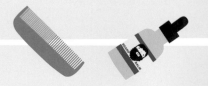

Finally, Elf starts to sew
a **sequin** *beard* that **gleams** and **glows**.

MERRY CHRISTMAS